THE BOY WHO W BROUGHT UP BY TEDDY BEARS

A fairy tale by **Jeanne Willis**

with pictures by **Susan Varley**

Ⓐ

Andersen Press · London

Once there was a little boy
who was brought up by Teddy Bears.
They found him in the woods, in his pram,
when he was a baby.

"Where's his mother?" wondered Big Teddy.
"Where's his father?" wondered Middle Teddy.
"I can't see them anywhere!" said Little Teddy.
So, thinking the baby was all alone in the world,
they carried him back to their cottage.

When they got home, the baby began to cry.
"He's hungry. Let's give him some sawdust," said Big Teddy.
"He's thirsty. Let's give him some pond water," said Middle Teddy.
"He's lonely. Let's give him a name," said Little Teddy.

They didn't know any People Names,
so they gave him Teddy names instead.
"I shall call him Pinky, because he's pink," said Big Teddy.
"I shall call him Blinky, because he blinks," said Middle Teddy.
"And I shall call him Dinky," said Little Teddy,
"because he's so little."

The Teddy Bears weren't sure whether to keep him or not.

"I think I should take him to the police," said Big Teddy.
"I think I should take him to hospital," said Middle Teddy.
"I think I should take him to bed," said Little Teddy.
Little Teddy got into bed and cuddled the baby
and it smiled and went fast to sleep.

The days turned into weeks . . .

. . . the weeks turned into years,
and all this time Pinky Blinky Dinky
was looked after by Teddy Bears.

He walked like a Teddy. He growled like a Teddy.
He could even swivel his legs all the way around . . . almost.

Grrrr

He slept in cupboards . . .

He sat on shelves . . .

He went to more picnics than you've had hot dinners.

He even dressed like a Teddy
and tied a red ribbon round his neck
with an enormous bow at the front.

And, of course, he was very cuddly.

For three whole years,
Pinky Blinky Dinky truly believed
he was a Teddy Bear.
"We have to tell him the truth,"
said Big Teddy.
"It might upset him,"
said Middle Teddy.
"He'll find out soon enough,"
said Little Teddy.

And so he did. On Pinky's fourth birthday,
there was a knock at the door.
It was his real mother.

"I'm searching for my long lost son," she said.
"He vanished from his pram when he was a baby.
Do you think the fairies might have taken him?"

"It wasn't the fairies," said Big Teddy.
"It was someone else," said Middle Teddy.
"It was us . . ." said Little Teddy.

And sure enough, there was Pinky Blinky Dinky,
lying with his legs in the air, upside down on the Teddy Bears' sofa!

"Edward!"
cried his mother. "My boy!"
"What's a boy?" said Pinky.
His mother tried to explain.

"But I don't want to be a boy!" he said.
"I want to be a Teddy Bear. I want to hide in cupboards
and go on picnics and play in the woods with my friends."
"Boys are allowed to do those things too," said his mother.
"But are boys allowed to have . . . cuddles?" he asked.
"Oh yes!" said his mother and she gave him
the biggest bear hug he'd ever had.

"I wish I could have a hug like that,"
sighed Big Teddy.
"So do I," said Middle Teddy.
"Me too!" said Little Teddy.

"Come here then," said Mum.
And she cuddled them all the way home.